Dragon Loves Penguin

Debi Gliori

BLOOMSBURY
LONDON

It's bedtime in the land of ice and snow.
"Night, night," says Bib's mummy.
"Sleep tight," says Bib's daddy.

But Bib has a better plan.
"Please . . . " says Bib,
"can I have a story?
The one about the dragons."

"Oh, Bib," sighs his mummy,
"just one story, and then
it's night, night, sleep tight."

"Don't let the frost bite,"
says Bib, snuggling in.

Dragon Loves
Penguin

"Long, long ago," Mummy begins,
"long before you hatched, dragons
came to live in our land of ice and snow.

They had lived all over the Earth,
from East to West and all points in between,
but nowhere seemed just right.
East was too . . . Easty,
West was the same . . . but Westish
and the points in between
were uncomfortably pointy."

"So the dragons arrived in the icy vastness
of our land and set up camp."

"Did they have tents and sleeping bags
in their camp?" asks Bib.

"I think they forgot to bring any," says Mummy.
"So, to keep warm they made their home
on top of a mountain with a fire in its heart
and there they spent the long, long winter,
waiting for spring."

"Sometimes it felt as if spring would never return,
but slowly the dark skies turned blue
and drip by drip, the ice began to thaw.

At last, the sun returned to the frozen land.

The dragons loved the sun.
They stretched their long necks,
spread their wide wings, and
polished their hard, shiny scales."

"Soon after that the eggs started coming.

Eggs with spots,
dots and stripes.

Eggs with lumps,
bumps and frills.

Some of the dragons laid little eggs,
some of them laid huge ones.

But one dragon, having no egg at all,
went off to be alone for a while."

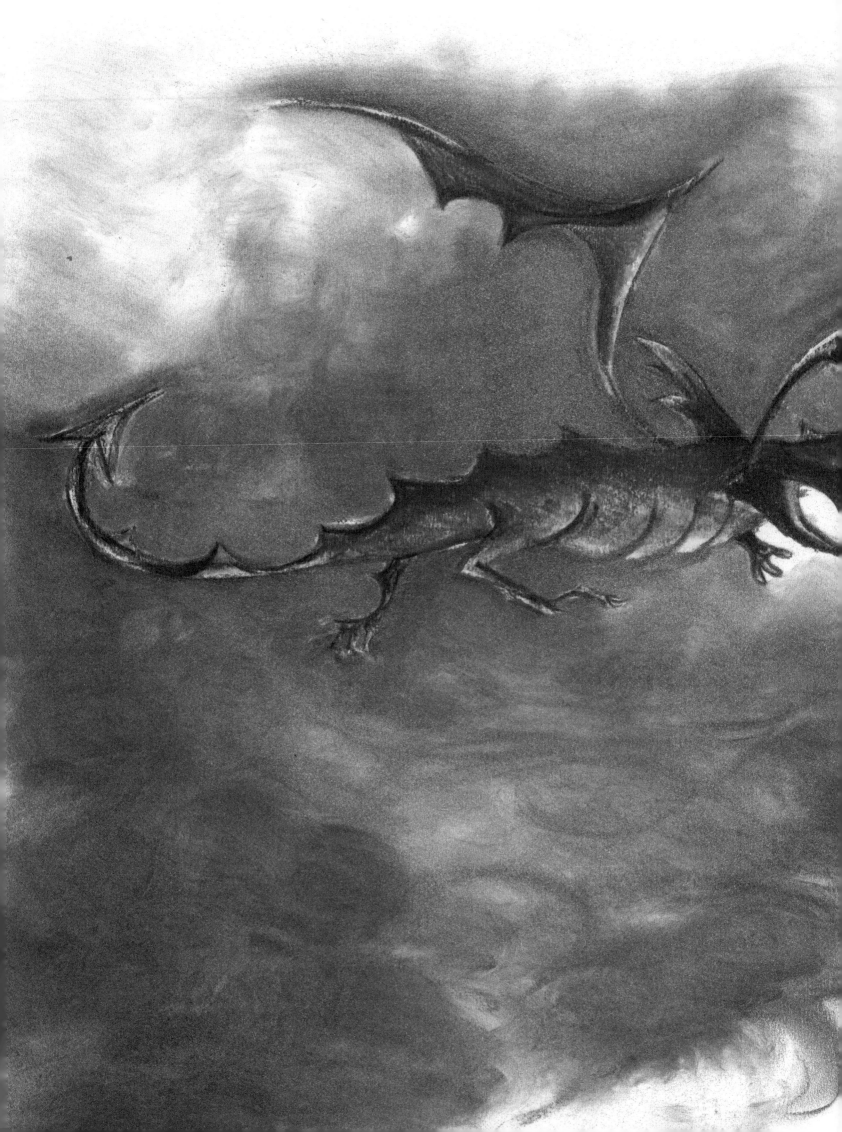

"Poor dragon," says Bib.
"I know," says Bib's mummy, "but . . .
sometimes things happen for a reason. Look."
"Oh!" gasps Bib, "poor *egg*."

"Yes," continues Bib's mummy, "that egg needed a mummy.

And that dragon needed an egg.

It was a perfect fit.

The dragon loved her Little One
through ice and sun.

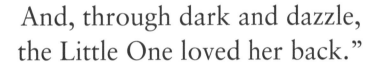

And, through dark and dazzle,
the Little One loved her back."

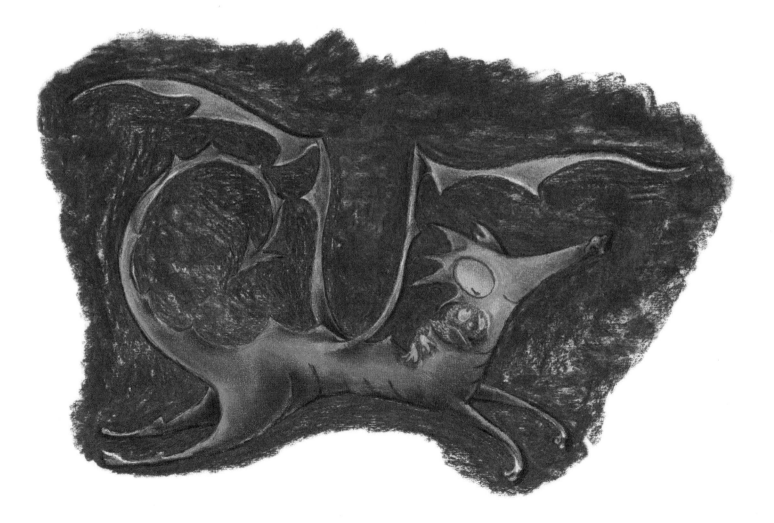

"All the other eggs were
quick to learn.

How to fly,

and breathe fire,

and chew rocks.

But the Little One
was slow and careful,
and learned to survive.

All the other eggs grew big and strong.
They grew long necks and wide wings
and hard scales all over.

But the Little One, being small
and fluffy, grew courage instead.

All the other eggs were given endless gifts –
fast toys; vast toys; flashing,
clattering things that made a noise.
But the Little One was given
love and time, the greatest gifts of all."

"Then one day, the big dragons had to go
far away to do big, important things.
Left behind, the small dragons grew fretful and cross.
They picked fights with each other.
Then they turned on the Little One.

'You're not a proper dragon,' they sneered. 'You can't fly.'
'You can't breathe fire.'
'You're covered in feathers, you big . . . softy.'"

"We're covered in feathers," says Bib.
"Yes," says Mummy, "feathers keep us warm,
but they can't keep cold words out."

"Feeling hurt and sad, the Little One
went away to be alone for a while.

Sometimes, things happen for a reason.

A real dragon's skin is too scaly to feel the heat,
but a soft, feathery dragon can feel the
first fiery breath when a volcano wakes up.

'FLEE FOR YOUR LIVES!'
the Little One screamed,
'THE MOUNTAIN IS ALIVE!'

The small dragons didn't wait to be told twice.
They didn't wait for the Little One either."

"The Little One tried to fly, but her wings were too small.

She tried to run, but the flames ran faster.

She screamed for help, but nobody heard.

Then she fell over, onto her soft,
feathery tummy.

Which was exactly
the right thing to do . . . "

"Down the mountain she went,
faster and faster,
sliding on her tummy,
all the way
to the bottom . . .

where she found something waiting for her.

An egg!"

"The egg was very small
but the Little One had more
than enough courage for
both of them.

And thanks to her mummy,
the Little One knew how to
survive through days of dark
and dazzle and ice and sun.

And later,
when the egg hatched,
who do you think was inside?"

"ME!" squeaks Bib.
"YOU!" says Mummy.

"I was the egg and
you were the
Little One!" says Bib.
"YES," says Mummy.

"And I knew the best gifts to give you.
Time and love.
Just like my dragon mummy gave me.
And now it's time to snuggle down."

"Read it again," says Bib. "Please?"

"Maybe Granny will tell you
the story this time," says Mummy.

"Please, please, please," says Bib,
"the dragon one.
About you, and Mummy, and me?"

"Snuggle down," says Granny,
"Close your eyes and I'll begin.
Long, long ago,
long before you hatched . . ."

For my Dragons, with love ~ DG

Bloomsbury Publishing, London, New Delhi, New York and Sydney

First published in Great Britain in 2013 by Bloomsbury Publishing Plc
50 Bedford Square, London, WC1B 3DP

This paperback edition first published in 2014

Text & illustrations copyright © Debi Gliori 2013

The moral right of the author/illustrator has been asserted

A CIP catalogue record for this book is available from the British Library

ISBN 978 1 4088 3949 2(HB)
ISBN 978 1 4088 3950 8 (PB)
ISBN 978 1 4088 3948 5 (eBook)

1 3 5 7 9 10 8 6 4 2

Printed in China by Leo Paper Products, Heshan, Guangdong

www.bloomsbury.com
www.debiglioribooks.com

All papers used by Bloomsbury Publishing are natural, recyclable products
made from wood grown in well-managed forests.
The manufacturing processes conform to the environmental regulations of the country of origin

BLOOMSBURY is a registered trademark of Bloomsbury Publishing Plc